TINY WORLDS

VOLUME ONE

J. CURTIS

———

<u>Attribution</u>

Select quotes from *Breakfast of Champions*, appear courtesy of Penguin Random House Publishing, Copyright 1973.

The following song lyrics included which constitute fair use under Section 107 of the Copyright Act of 1976. The song lyrics are the property of their respective owners.

- *Good Hearted Woman* by Waylon Jennings and Willie Nelson
- *Space Oddity* by David Bowie

For my family –

You crazy, lovely souls who endure my nonsense every day.

For new stories, visit TinyWorlds.substack.com

CONTENTS

FOREWORD

In the preface of his book *Breakfast of Champions*, Kurt Vonnegut had this to say about reaching 50 years old:

"This book is my fiftieth-birthday present to myself. I feel as though I am crossing the spine of a roof—having ascended one slope. I am programmed at fifty to perform childishly..."

Vonnegut then goes on to discuss assholes, including a picture of one he has drawn with a felt-tipped pen.

I think that's a fitting start here, too.

This book, the one in your hands, is a gift for *my* 50th birthday. Unlike Vonnegut at the time of *BoC*, I don't have six novels completed. I have, at a quick glance, a few dozen stories with more in the hopper. Oh, and a novel in progress—but what writer doesn't have one or ten of those?

The stories and writerly sketches in *Volume One* vary in length, ranging from a few hundred to a few thousand words. Brevity, the sages tell me, is paramount to keeping the reader (and writer) engaged. And, keeping with the Tiny theme, the paperback version should fit comfortably into a carry-on or purse, so it can be surreptitiously left among other, more recognizable books at a holiday rental house.

A few stories include a soundtrack notation. These tracks are ones I listened to while writing or editing. I've found that sometimes a simple piece of music can buttress the words or take the reader on a new path. You may disagree with my choice, and I suppose we'll both have to live with that grudge between us.

Though brief, these stories aren't without substance. In them, I hope you'll find moments that make you smile, cringe, or even pause to reflect on the world around us. They're meant, as the title implies, to capture tiny moments—whole worlds or scenes that beg our attention, if only we'd look.

And finally, at no point will I offer hand-rendered illustrations, felt-tipped or otherwise. Promise.

-J. Curtis

Adapted from **Tiny Worlds | Dispatch No. 1**

1. PAID-IN-FULL

CHIRP. BUZZ.

My phone vibrated.

My left eye barely opened.

A text message: *"You need to get moving!"*

I didn't recognize the number and responded with a "?"

CHIRP. BUZZ. *"Get up!"*

I blink at the phone, puzzled. Sigh. My alarm wasn't set to go off for another hour.

"You have 2 minutes to get out!"

I sit up. The cat isn't on the bed but she's mewing from the hallway. Probably hungry.

Holding the phone in one hand, I pull on a t-shirt from the dirty laundry and pad to the living room. Police sirens sounded in the distance. Still dark. I hate winter.

"1 minute. Go outside!"

The cat meets me at the side door, clawing at the wood. When I open it, a blast of cold wind stands my nipples erect and retracts my balls. This happens with equal speed and shock.

The sirens grow louder as I lean out to look around. The cat has darted away into the darkness.

"Walk to the oak tree."

The grass is wet underfoot and I high step quickly as if that could keep my feet dry. A snail crunches under the ball of my foot, its guts oozing between my toes. I swipe at the ground to remove it.

A car turns the corner, tires squealing, sirens chasing. It's getting louder. Both eyes are open now but I'm briefly blinded. Red and blue flashes light up the hedges as I see two cars careening down the street.

The lead car picks up speed. The cat runs out, pausing in the middle of the street. It seems uncertain which way to go.

I catch a glimpse–the first driver spots the cat. He swerves. The cat changes direction. Not enough time for the driver to react, but he tries. His wheels bounce as he mounts the curb. I think I see sparks. I definitely hear grinding then a crunch as it plows hood-first into my house.

A car is parked in my home. Inside *my* bedroom. The accelerator must be stuck because its wheels are spinning on my mattress.

A police car slides to a stop on the lawn, lights flashing. Red. Blue. Red. Blue. Everything looks like a 3D movie from the 60s, without glasses.

Two cops race across the lawn. They shout at the house and at the car, I guess, but nobody answered.

I'm still not fully awake. A piece of snail shell scrapes between my toes.

CHIRP. BUZZ. *"You're safe?"*

I look, blinking at the words, and type: "Yes. Who is this?"

"Look across the street."

I squint and see a man standing in the shadows beneath a tree. He holds up his phone for a moment, then goes back to typing, "..."

"I'm Theo, your insurance agent. Because your homeowner policy was current, we extended a one-time, limited-use Future Insurance policy on your behalf. Consider this portion paid-in-full. I'll send a regular adjuster for the rest."

"..."

"Have a great day!"

The cat crosses the street toward me and begins mewing.

She's always hungry.

————

Music to read by: <u>The Moonbeam Song</u> by Harry Nilsson

2. THE PUNGENT PARADOX OF AFFECTION

Oh gawd, you again?
I saw you hiding, pretending I don't exist
we both can smell your stench.
Don't think I can't...because I can.
You're disgracefully amazing

Last Tuesday, when we were together
remember that dinner?
It's not like you own the place
but everyone in the restaurant thinks you do

The waiters smiled
and everyone around just looked at you
...wait, how did they look at you?
Lovingly?
They all fucking love you

I hate you.
I can't stand to be near you.

But, you know I'm drawn to you.

I want you around.
I want to feel you on my lips,
my tongue

I want you and only you,
everywhere
I want you in my kitchen,
next to me,
under my nails.

I want you in the back yard,
beneath the trees,
in the shade
so we both don't burn in our nakedness.

My skin is thinner than yours
I can't stay away

You control and repulse me
You offend my friends
...my dates
...the Fedex guy

Are you free next Wednesday?
I love you, garlic.

3. SOMEBODY'S GOING
TO JAIL

"GOOD MAGICIANS DON'T DO A TRICK TWICE," SHE says, giving him a slow blink.

Leaning, a man in a button-up shirt, who truly believes it's 5 O'clock somewhere, has his sport coat off. He's trying to get comfortably close. Probably a salesman, she thinks. He'd tell her everything about some damned widget if only she'd ask.

"Oh, c'mon..." the salesman pleads, nudging her drink. He thinks she might be a local with her southern drawl. He, on the other hand, is Midwestern. To him, she seems exotic, and maybe easy, too.

Voices croon from across the spill-proof concrete floor, *"She loves me in spite of my wicked ways that she don't understand..."* Waylon and Willie know that outlaw cowboys have their own kind of appeal.

A lone dart dangles, thrown wide of the board and buried in mottled paneling. Any patron would have a hard time not smelling the beer, blood, piss, and smoke baked into a dive like this.

The salesman motions to the bartender to come over. There are only three of them in the place, but he makes an effort of it —"She says she's got a story that'll make you piss your pants."

The bartender looks between them and starts his count: 1 point for lazy eyes, 2 points for slurred speech, 1 point for each double of cheap whiskey between them for the last hour. 1 + 2 + 4. There's no tip coming.

"I've heard 'em all," the bartender sighs, taking a peep at his watch.

"Like you know anything about comedy," the woman says, snapping her gum at the bartender.

"Only that it's all about timing. I lock the door in five minutes."

The salesman grabs for his wallet, "Maybe one more?"

She puts a hand on the salesman's shoulder, "I'm good, sugar. We'll be out of here soon," she winks.

Soon is good—he blinks.

The woman turns, smiles faintly at the bartender then to the salesman, flapping her doe eyes. She sticks her gum to the lip of the glass, stirs it with a pinky. Ice jingles.

"Yes, comedy is all about timing. But stories set a mood," she says. "Anyway, you got me in a mood, so I'll tell ya."

The salesman: primed after the second drink, he'd pay attention to anything with tits.

The bartender has seen it all: the lonesome out-of-towner, the local floozy, too many drinks, a sudden rush out the door. But, he thinks, she does have a nice shade of lipstick.

Seeing she's got their attention, she licks her lips, touches the corners of her mouth with a finger before she runs her hands along her dress.

"My uncle walked into a bar like this'n. He had himself a good night out. That was his thing 'cause he was from Macon, and there ain't shit to do there but drink. But he walks in and slaps down his last ten dollars. He shouts at the barman—" The woman leans to the bartender and yells, "Cheapest shit that'll get me arrested!"

The bartender doesn't budge. She smiles an apology, taps the edge of his nose, and continues.

"The barman, who looked a bit like you, steps up and pours my uncle a tall glass of everything that fell into the bar mat. Just turned it upside down until every last drop of everything that spilled the whole night filled that glass. Now, my uncle, not one to turn down a dare of any sort, takes this as a challenge. He rises up on his barstool and points his finger in the chest of the barman and says, 'How about I race you around the block after this has taken hold?'"

The salesman pats his palms on the curved edge bar. His face is bright all around his whiskey eyes, his bottom lip curled up under his teeth.

"Thinking he had my uncle, the barman says, 'I'll take that bet, but I get to choose the course.'"

The bartender follows the salesman, leaning in. It's all about to come to a head, and they want a front-row seat, such as it is.

The woman pauses her story. She reaches out and snap-points at the bowl of peanuts down the bar. The salesman blinks, caught unaware. The bartender slides it in front of her.

"There was a crowd that night, and everyone lined up to watch."

She rummages through the bowl of unshelled peanuts — too bumpy, too small. She selects one and flips it open like a Zippo, throwing the bare peanuts into her mouth, making a show of it, and smiles.

"They agreed to go out the bar, through the parking lot, through a hole in the fence, and back inside. First to touch the bar wins."

She looks between them, positioning herself, "You gentlemen interested in a race?"

The music fades away as the two men lock eyes, each sizing up the other.

Giving a wink, she says, tapping her hips, "I'll be the bar."

She has the spotlight. And men, well, men are stupid. She can see that time doesn't matter to the bartender now. The salesman, he's been hers from the go.

Their silence is her answer.

"Now, gentlemen, before I tell this last part, I need you both to promise me something..."

The two men lean, listening closely. Pausing, she looks at them both, turning her head side to side, cracking her neck. She downs the rest of her drink and, saving the gum from the edge, pops it back into her mouth. She pops it, turning mock serious.

"I swear it's worth it. But If you want to play along, I've got rules so nobody does anything stupid. I mean it. Someone's gonna holler and someone's probably going to jail when I finish."

Hands go up; they both feign a non-threatening posture. They like the game. She smiles at them both and looks around. The dart still dangles and there isn't another soul in the place.

She looks at the bartender and motions, "You go stand over there in that open area."

Then, the salesman stands up. She plants a long kiss on his lips. His hands are at his sides but quickly move to her hips.

"Honey, you go stand over by the door," she whispers in his ear, "It'll make for a quicker exit."

She can see the bartender over the salesman's shoulder. She looks him up and down and sends an air kiss. The salesman finds his spot as she makes her way to the middle of the room, just about equal distance between the men.

"The crowd is whoopin' and hollerin'. Everyone in that town knew my uncle. My uncle says to the bartender, 'It's a sporting thing to do to let the challenger say when.' So they nodded to each other and hunker down, stretching like it was the Olympics. This was going to be a tight race—that barman was All American, and my uncle, even in his inebriated state, was no slouch — he'd been known to outrun most of the town cops at one time or another."

She pulls a tube of lipstick from her bra. "Sorry fellas, a lady has to keep her appearances."

Tilting her head back, pouting, she strokes the lipstick thickly. Both men watch lasciviously as she blots top lip to bottom and rolls the lipstick down, slipping it neatly back into her bra.

"The barman started the countdown, 'On your mark...'"

The salesman licks the perspiration from his upper lip. The bartender twitches.

"Get Set..."

Both men are poised. They're racehorses a few years past prime, breathing hard and ready. Her long lashes rise and fall as her eyes flit between the bartender and the salesman.

She reaches down, pulling up the hem of her dress. They watch every motion: her knees, her stockings, the edge of a garter. The corner of her mouth turns up; she's got them both. Then, the edge of a leather holster – a revolver.

"Go!"

She spins like lightning toward the salesman and fires! His eyes go wide. The bullet sings past, putting a dent in the metal door behind him. He screams! Everyone is deaf.

The woman walks toward the salesman, gun pointed at him. He's dumbfounded, mouth slack. She talks loud over the ringing in their ears.

"My uncle ran his ass off that night..."

She fires again, splintering the wood on the door jam.

"Out of the bar..."

The salesman gets the hint; he whips the door open and spins out onto the pavement.

"Through the parking lot..."

The salesman is sputtering, scraping at the ground, trying to move faster than his body will let him. He's a cartoon set loose out into the cold night. His arms are pumping. He looks back at the doorway and sees but doesn't see. The woman gets to the door just as he runs past a hole in the fence at the edge of the parking lot.

She smiles. There's a sound behind her. She turns to see the bartender walking toward her. She points the gun squarely at his chest. He's not stopping; she grips the handle, her finger on the trigger.

"You're going to jail," the bartender says, "again."

She reaches back and flips the lock on the door without looking. He grabs her wrists and pins her arms against the door.

"Oh, love. You know we've got 20 minutes before the cops get here—"

She licks her lips. The red of the lipstick shines. It's his favorite shade.

———

Music to read by: <u>Good Hearted Woman</u> by Waylon Jennings & Willie Nelson

4. MR. UNREASONABLY CHEERY FLOWERS

"Whoo-boy," Larry says as he studies the flowers. It takes him a minute, then a few steps back to gather the whole of it in view. Enormous. Gargantuan. Panoramic. A Preakness wreath. When was the last time he even bought flowers? Even his mother got day-old croissants from the bakery, not a bouquet. And what, exactly, was the etiquette for a canine wake?

The size was one thing, but the colors made it unsettling, too. From phone call to reality, the bouquet had transformed from "nice but somber" to "Golden Girls-esque." This bouquet was a damned Floridian habitat. The size, he found, was further complemented by its price.

Getting that monstrosity through a door was like giving birth to Latin America. It was hastily followed by the arctic face slap of winter in New York. *Bienvenido, jerk off!*

Larry winced at the wind and teetered his way toward a nearby bus stop. Wads of wet snow fell around Larry and his, he began to think, unreasonably cheery flowers.

"*Aunt Bea,*" he muttered aloud, "*I'm sorry for your loss. Here's something...festive?*" It sounded worse out loud.

But the Yorkie, Aunt Bea's "little mister," was doted on like a child. For God's sake, she dressed it as a leprechaun for St. Patrick's Day and took it to Sunday mass in a handmade suit. This dog was Aunt Bea's life. Were flowers really the answer? *These* flowers?

The sidewalk in front of the bus stop, visible through spikes of bottle brush, looked empty. Cowards, he thought, they're all crammed under the shelter. Narrowing his eyes, he searched for a way under the structure, out of the chill. Larry considered flanking through the street—bumper-to-bumper cars, a panhandler tapping on windows, and a gutter full of slush. Not a great option among them.

Larry tisked, running his tongue over his teeth. With a firm shoulder and agile footwork, he did what New Yorkers do best: ignore and push through. He grunted a "*pardon me*" to the responding "*whatchits*" from smashed toes or jostled groceries. Dodge, parry, juke. Deep in the warmth of the crowd, Larry rolled his shoulders and neck in triumph. Like a conqueror. He smiled behind the foliage.

Aunt Bea would not have been proud. She would have wagged her gnarled finger at him and said, "*We're better than that, Lawrence. We don't crowd people.*" Larry would swallow hard but want to say, "This is Queens, not Sheep Meadow. Go there and get all the space you want for blankets and picnics and dogs."

Because that's where she would go: afternoons on a blanket with the only things that truly mattered—his mother, Aunt Bea, and their Yorkies. Their own little dog day afternoon.

Over the crowd, Larry saw traffic inching along. Would there still be time? He shifted the weight of the vase (planter!) to shore his grip. It's growing heavier by the second, isn't it? This subtropical cascade of friendliness is too wide to see his own watch. He searched for someone, anyone, using a phone. Not a single craned neck. "What century is this?" he thought.

Then, plop, pleep, plip. Drips fell from the canopy, slaloming down his face. It's maddening. He was about to lose it and run screaming...until he saw his reflection in the glass. Gadzooks, you Einstein! Use the reflection to check your watch!

Larry shifted, turned enough to catch sight of his sleeve. He shrugged, pulling back his cuff. Up it goes, then a bit more— not quite far enough. He tried again. The sleeve pulled up enough for him to see the hour hand. Shrug-pull-roll, then the minute hand!

Gah! An eternal three minutes had elapsed. Yes, there's still time. But, really, what idiot holds a service on a Wednesday? Then, Larry remembered—Aunt Bea. She would have frowned at him, her sigh breezing past the wisps of dark hair that sometimes nested on her upper lip. Wednesday would be when Father Whathis-name has time to say a few prayers, spin the rosary, whatever.

Stuck. Trapped. But crisis averted, Larry's breathing slowed. He blew back stray hairs on his forehead, regaining compo-sure. To prove it, he winked at his reflection. Is that a blotch on his tie? He looked down. Mustard? No, the casserole he devoured over the sink. A spot wouldn't matter on ordinary ties, but this silk tie, a gift from Aunt Bea, was special.

"You take care of this and it'll take care of you," she had told him. And he did, mostly. This tie had its own hanger. That counted for something, right?

The group pulled closer, avoiding the cold. Constricted to his stance, Larry was helpless to clean the tie. Or was he? He tilted his chin down, wondering if it's closer than it looks.

His eyes darted left, then right—no one was looking.

Arcing his neck with great effort, his tongue reached for the stained necktie. His chins multiplied as his tongue stretched and his shoulders hunched. *Ahmmmm—mhmmm.* He wedged his chin under the collar, lifting the tie, closing the distance. Then, he felt it. The wind shifted, suddenly warmer.

Tongue out, he turned his head to see the woman next to him, staring. She might be a foot away, but her eyeballs were practically touching his. Larry froze. She didn't blink. He blushed, pulled his tongue back, and gave the woman a slow shrug. His face said, *Whaddayagonnado?*

She's still staring. Her eyes, he thought, might be crazy.

He didn't want to look, but surely this isn't the craziest thing she's seen on a Wednesday. Their eyes locked. He turned his head to face the traffic, and she followed suit. They kept each other in their peripheral vision, past the whites of their eyes and around the crow's feet. Larry looked forward, then back at her. She met his gaze again. He maintained eye contact, nodded toward the street, and cleared his throat. She followed his motion.

And this, this Aunt Bea would have loved to see. She might have crossed herself two or three times, but she'd have watched it like the Westminster Kennel Club.

The brave panhandler Larry saw earlier rounded a row of cars close to them. He wore a long, ragged overcoat and woolen mittens. With a Fosse-perfect move, he put his hands in his coat pockets and slid effortlessly on the snow. What moves,

Larry thought. He looked like he's floating, drifting the length of the gutter, letting the overcoat flow in the wind. It was picturesque. Underneath the overcoat—no pants, no underwear, no shame. And from this moment on, Larry thought, this fella owns the award for cold weather adaptability. The woman's stare never returned. This is New York, after all; there's always something better to gawk at.

The snow, still falling in clumpy balls of yeti shit, squished as the bus rolled up. Larry could hear the sound of squeaking shoes on the wet stairs as he moved with the crowd. Like little Yorkie feet in plastic rain boots. That made him laugh, thinking of Aunt Bea bundling up her Yorkie in a little knitted coat she had made herself. *"A gentleman must be properly dressed,"* she'd say with a wink. The Yorkie would trot along, looking proud as ever, his tiny coat matching Bea's.

It'll probably have a casket, Larry thought, a miniature one. The dog is likely to be dressed up in a sequined suit she made, too. Celebratory. Garish. Like the flowers.

Larry remembered not to trip as he stepped over the hill of snow. The white of it hadn't given up just yet. It was mostly gray now, the color of Bea's Yorkie. Her *former* Yorkie.

This stuff, it's wet but you could hardly call it snow. Slush, maybe. If these flowers don't do the trick, Larry thought, we can scoop up this slush, toss it in a cone with syrup, and serve it at the dog funeral. Now that's a proper send-off.

———

Music to read by: "Place To Be" by Nick Drake

5. FIONA

Fiona whispered, "Over here!" to start the game. She cupped her hands and listened. Any second now, she would hear rustling in her parents' room, followed by sleepy groans, blankets flung wide, and the patter of footsteps on the old wooden floor. She'd respond with her own mighty four-year-old elephant stomps, echoing through the hall.

On cue, her parents burst from their bedroom, nightgowns fluttering, their faces worn with another night of lost sleep and whispered pleas. Fiona took great delight in her mischievous play — sometimes early, too early, before the sun was up. By breakfast, her game would be over, the morning wind carrying the sweet scent of alfalfa and huckleberries that lined the fields.

Twilight was Fiona's realm. After all, she'd never feared the dark. Inky shadows pooled between lamps, perfect hiding spots for her small frame. Her parents' whispers echoed, but she'd only taunt them with a hushed, "Over here!" before vanishing into another room. She'd stifle a giggle, hand pressed to her mouth.

From the darkness, she watched them creep, their exhausted faces barely visible in the gloom. But Fiona could hear their every breath, see their blinking eyes searching in vain.

Of all the games, hide and seek was Fiona's favorite. It started last autumn when the chill drove them indoors. Mother would spin and spin, eyes shut tight, until the room blurred into a whirl of shapes. Then, Fiona would scramble, her feet unsteady with excitement, searching every corner of the drafty house. It was a glorious maze, and she'd dash through the halls, breathless until – finally! – she'd find her mother. They'd collapse in a heap of laughter, Fiona already begging, "Again! Again!"

But now the game was Fiona's. With each play, she became more inventive. She'd lead them on a spirited chase—a whirlwind up the front stairwell, then a scramble back down. Sometimes she'd clatter pots in the kitchen or splash in the parlor fountain, leaving a trail of wet handprints. Darting across the polished music room, she'd be careful not to let the sliding doors bang together.

The attic, with its deep dust and disordered shapes of boxes, was ideal but her parents had forbidden its use. As was the cold, musty root cellar and the ornamental garden outside. None of that mattered to Fiona who was pleased to play inside the house with its many floors and rooms. She was diligent and always took note of new alcoves or cubbies to hide every time they played. Even when her parents changed the rules by locking doors Fiona always found a way inside.

Down the dark hallway her feet would pad, parents close in chase, and into her bedroom where she'd slam the door and peer through the keyhole watching them approach. Her parents knew her game, calling out, "Fiona, where are you?"

But Fiona was too good. Even as they approached, laughter bubbled up inside her, a giggle threatening to escape but held back by her hands tightly pressed over her mouth. She'd never give away her location. Motionless as a statue, she hides behind the tall, heavy curtains.

She hears her father enter, her mother's soft voice would call out, "Fiona, come back to me." The curtains hastily swept open, revealing only a moonlit window and the village below. Her mother sank onto the bed, her fingers tracing the dusty photo of four-year-old Fiona.

Eyes shut, Fiona held back the giggle that threatened to burst free. Tomorrow, they'd play again. And again. And again.

6. MEL'S MARBLE

MEL'S RASPY WHOOP WAS CONTAGIOUS AS HE pumped his knees like he was doing a rain dance. Even the boys on the sidewalk rolled over, bellies fluttering with uncontrollable giggles. Mel earned that win.

The game was everything, and this one was serious – double elimination, best marbles only. We set the lineup with inka-binka, then rock-paper-scissors, just to be doubly-sure who would go first. Each of us chose the best from our collection: maybe an aggie, a cat's eye, a zombie, a galaxy, or a troll. No steelies allowed.

The twins were out before the sun was overhead, divvying up an oriole for the winner. Then, Mel took a beating. He was tending store so we let him play a bit of slop when he had time. We all took turns being referee, whispering if a shot was legal – like a dink or a smidge. Some older boys stepped in our game, maybe tow-head's hood brother. But Mel ran 'em off. He was always looking out for us.

We couldn't imagine a better way to stave off the heat of a July afternoon. Here, under the awning of the Vine Street Market our bottles of cream soda stayed cold as we played for hours. Sitting on the ground, our cuffs and collars would be spoilt. Getting a finger-wag from your mother was worth it.

The tow-head kid who lived next to the big maple was on a streak. He'd look right through you without blinking. We weren't afraid of him, though. That boy's shots were wild, spinning and tumbling the wrong way until the very last moment. Then, like a gunslinger he'd hold his arms in front and pretend to pull an imaginary trigger. Grabbing our chests we'd fall to the ground, laughing. Sooner or later, it was just him and Mel.

Mel brought out his best marble: a Milky Way. It had a white outer layer and the bluest, speckled inner you'd ever seen. He usually shot from a crouch, but with shadows growing long, his close-in game was better on the ground. Pretending to block the sun from his patched eye, he squinted like a sniper with the other.

Usually, he'd shoot with his left hand if he was just messing with us. But not now, not with his best marble at stake. His right arm extended out as he curled his fingers, bird meeting thumb. We held our breath as his hand twisted to find the best angle. Too much English, and the shot would spoil; too little, and he'd miss.

His flick was silent and precise, finger barely touching the glass – even the marble was surprised. Skimming over the grit, it wobbled and bounced. We rose on our elbows for a better view. Everyone inhaled the humid air, holding it. The glass galaxy weaved and tapped the edge of another marble. A rico-chet! Yowza! Mel's marble spun back toward the center and knocked the other just over the chalk.

We erupted! Mel hooted and danced around the circle on one leg as if he were our age. Reaching down, he swiped both marbles from the ground and gave 'em a spit polish with his untucked shirt. I thought the tow-head kid was going to cry. Mel was too kind to keep both, so he handed the other marble back.

Under the awning, we all shared another soda as Mel, pleased as punch, locked up and turned out the store sign. He waved goodbye, winking with his one good eye. We heard his whistling from the next block long after he was out of sight.

———

They spend the morning looking at Want Ads at the diner. A shared plate of french fries between them doesn't last long but you can't beat the price of bottomless coffee.

Opposites, like sugar and salt. One, a greasy blonde, leans over the newspaper. The other meaty, a butch cut above a scatter of freckles on either side of his pig nose.

"What do you know about working at a grain elevator?" the blonde boy says. An earnest question, if rhetorical, to the other across the booth.

"'Bout as much as you know about girls," the other boy says. His attention is focused on the mostly empty plate, giving no mind to sounds that come from his mouth. Forgettable words might be as good a trait as any he has.

"Can't be all that hard, right? Just need a strong back. I got that."

A grunt. Dabbing the last of the fries, meaty fingers slide in a puddle of ketchup.

"My old man's gonna boot me if I don't find a job," the rumpled newspaper twists and folds.

"He's been saying that for a year."

"He means it – says all my stuff is gonna be piled in the lawn by sundown."

The pig licks the plate. He washes the ketchup down with the last of his coffee and looks around for the waitress. He thinks he'll have another cup.

"I know where easier money is made."

They drive, the meaty boy behind the wheel – across town, past the park. It is his idea and the Buick is *his* car. He never lets anyone else behind the wheel. He knows when to double-clutch the shift, when the engine will sputter with too much gas. Most of all, he's a hot shoe at the getaway.

"Here?" the blonde says as they roll up to the curb, "No way, I live just over there."

Behind the wheel, the meaty boy ignores the words, and the gesture to the creme house with the tall maple. Save for a patch of grass over the septic, the lawn is still dirt-empty.

From the back seat, the driver pulls a rusty meat tenderizer. It is heavy and oversized, ready-made for a butcher shop. He tests the weight leaving dimples in the heel of his hand with each thud.

"Fella's always got a drawer full of cash and only one eye. Just get him to turn around."

———

"Got ID?" Mel says, standing behind the counter.

Mel likes to keep the wide counter clear for customers, no need for all those chotchkies. That store on Main has junk everywhere, he thinks. Not his Vine Street Market; Mel keeps it button-neat. Tidy shelves with cereal and soup. His cooler is always stocked with milk and soda, even fresh fruit he gets from the orchard at the edge of town. Heck, even the hooch is well organized behind the counter. He knows his good customers appreciate cleanliness, too.

"You used to trade worms for bubble gum...long time ago," the blonde boy at the counter says, trying to make small talk. Mel blinks his eye, watching him. Mel knows his face, probably only a few years older than the boys outside. Probably still a teen though, judging by his leftover acne.

Mel nods, he remembers, "Never needed any other kind of bait."

The open counter lets Mel have a better look at people, like these two. Even with one eye, he can still size people up quickly. He's seen that old, pre-war Buick around town. Before the war might have been the last time it had a tune-up, too. Mel thinks it a shame to let things go to rust.

The other one, the heavier one, wanders the store. Mel watches him pick up a box of soup and pretend to read. Probably can't read, just looks at the pictures, he thinks. Damn shame we don't kick these kids back a grade. Or send 'em somewhere they'd get a real education. They'd be better after some time in a third world with only a rucksack and a pocket translator. No TV, no Saturday matinee cartoons – just your wits and the kindness of a stranger.

At the counter, the blonde leans in, his voice low, commiserating, "–must've forgot it. Next time?"

Mel glances at the clock above the door: 11:39. Still morning and a little early for a drink. Mel gives a half-smile that makes his eye patch move, "What kind did you say?"

"Oh – the bottle of, uh, Old Raven," the boy says, motioning to the shelves behind, shifting his weight forward, elbows on the counter, trying on nonchalance like a paper mustache.

Mel reaches a hand down below the counter, eye staying on the boy. From below he sets a bottle on the counter: Old Raven. Mel watches the boy's expression change, his jaw clenches before his tongue darts to the corner of his mouth, thinking.

"...must have been mistaken," the blonde says, pointing to the bottles on the shelf behind Mel, "Maybe I need glasses – what's the red label up there?"

Mel doesn't turn, he knows his inventory, "That's the expensive stuff. Maybe you want something else?"

From a back aisle, the meaty boy coughs, insistent. Mel studies the boy in front of him, watching him look at the shelf of liquor, lips inward, thinking, considering. The towhead kid outside sometimes does that when he shoots marbles. But this'n doesn't stare you down like the little one – a manner he didn't pick up from his daddy. No, this is the gentle one he'd hear crying on his way home, hiding up in the limbs of the maple tree. This is the one who got the bruises and a cigarette burn on his temple, which he hides with his hair.

Mel slides the Old Raven below the counter and leans forward, whisper-distance, "Your friend – is he the smart one, or are you?"

The blonde boy at the counter stops fidgeting, looks at Mel's good eye, listening, "Your daddy never gets the good stuff. But he's a hard worker. Maybe you are, too?"

The boy's face shifts, he senses something in Mel's steady voice. Then, he hears the other boy walking from the back of the store. Mel lowers his eye, focusing on the boy in front of him, looking just past his eyebrows, "Tomorrow. Honest work. Stock room needs help."

Footsteps approach behind, Mel's hand drops, his eye doesn't leave the boy at the counter, "Understand?" The boy nods, his blonde hair falling in his eyes.

Meaty hands pull the blonde aside, hand raised, holding the tenderizer, "Enough! Give me the cash old ma–"

A pistol, pointed at the meaty boy's center. Mel's hand is steady. Without a doubt, not even a one-eyed man would miss at this distance.

The boy's eyes go wide, meaty hands shoot up, dropping the tenderizer to the floor with a bang.

Mel says a clear, single, button-neat word: "Out!"

The larger boy backs away, his moves cautious until he gets near to the door. Both boys sprint out. Mel can hear the flapping of footsteps, then a shout from the boys outside. Mel listens, ears attuned – one car door, an engine, a second door. Finally, the sound of hammers colliding under the hood of the Buick as it squeals away.

Mel slides the pistol back under the counter before making his way down an aisle. He gently pushes the box of soup neatly back into place. Tidy.

Pausing in the stillness of the shop, Mel rubs his forehead. He scratches his cheek, his throat, his Adam's apple. He thinks he is due for a shave. Outside he can hear the boys playing, laughing. Someone missed a big shot and they're taunting each other.

Mel lifts his eye patch touching the glass eye underneath. He gives it a poke from the side as it drops into his hand. A Milky Way – a white outer layer and the bluest, speckled inner you've ever seen.

The bell on the door chimes as he exits into the full July heat. "Is it my turn yet?" he says.

———

Music to read by: <u>Papa Was A Rollin' Stone</u> by The Temptations

7. AUSTRALIA

This is what Frieda says nearly every day as she spreads the morning newspaper. Is it that often? Yeah, I recon. She'll go on forever or so if the earthquakes or wildfires don't catch her first. Heaven and Frieda know it won't be the wildlife but she'll get to that soon enough.

Her finger skims along the print, bottom to top, before reaching the headline. She flips and folds her paper creating parcels of words. She'll sit and absorb them for hours.

Without looking, she pours too much milk. I hate when coffee is the color of baby shit smeared on an ivory wall, but Freida does. Her spoon makes a dull clink on the ceramic. The mug is in a different key than the chimes hanging outside. Right now it's too chilly to open a window and hear them fully. Maybe later, when the afternoon wind brushes by and lets them ring true will be better.

After a long pause and a gulp Freida's yabber continues:

"Back home in Australia, damned-near everything has fangs or rabies – shrubs, sharks, jumping spiders and whatnot. They're ordained by God to make sure you don't get soft!"

She laughs a "ha!" at her own words. The ting of her hinterland accent is strongest in the morning. "Australia" is a side-mouthed lazy jumble. Freida's kin are known to wander daylong in a word where every vowel is blind drunk looking for a ride home. She'd never cop to it but I hear it.

Her mouth turns up and for a quick second I can see her teeth. She looks past the newspaper and coffee and cream, through the window and to the hummingbirds circling a feeder. It's the best smile she can muster but it's beautiful. I can almost tell what she's thinking. Frieda and her morning breath rock in the wicker chair. The coffee will tame it a bit but I keep my distance just the same.

8. THE MAGICIAN'S WIDOW

Black cars of sadness
line the street
a burial, now a reception
Brilliant flowers to lighten the mood
eyes stay turned to hands
and shoes and rugs

Till they met her eyes
bright
her veil removed
and voice steady
as the magician's widow
performs his last show

Well-wishers
replete with short sentences
remembrances heartfelt
tributes of rapport
from friend and also from foe

Surrounded by his livelihood

pictures and props
a lifetime of spectacle
attest his flourish, his skill
yet hide his secrets
as eyes wander
to the old wooden trunk

When the crowd finally wanes
the house empty by half
her eyes watch
stragglers and frauds
already knowing their tell
except the young girl
book at her lap

Kneeling
the widow palms a card
hiding a smirk as
the girl responds in kind
with a second, a match
the deuce of hearts

Bending and folding
cards twist, together
hearts become a key
and the trunk unlocks

9. PLACEBO

"Stop looking," she said aloud. **"Just take it already."**

Was it past midnight? She turned up her wrist to check her watch but didn't look. Did it matter? Her eyes couldn't leave the shape on the nightstand—a little half egg with diamond-like facets barely casting a shadow. It was light, probably plastic, and see-through. That's how she knew the pill was inside.

Her mind flashed to earlier, at the curb when the delivery truck arrived. It was the first time she'd left the house all day. The driver held out a pad to sign, handing her the box.

"It's exciting," she said to him. "To finally get something you've been waiting for all your life."

He shrugged and said, "That's a long time to wait, I guess."

The truck wasn't out of earshot before the package was unwrapped. Inside, she saw the decorative box. It was beautiful. Her fingers traced the red silk ribbon that wrapped it, reading the embossed silver text: *Tomorrow Everything Changes.*

She felt flush; a hot wave swept over her, blood rushed to pink her cheeks, sweat beading on her forehead. The familiar tingle of panic set in. It was how she felt on the train during rush hour—her chest tight, breathing shallow.

Or queuing at airport security, lips dry, the urge to pee. Or sometimes, even standing in line at the coffee shop, the feeling she might run out the door screaming. In those moments, she felt her insides warm to a boil, the pressure building, trapped and wanting to be free.

She had almost scrolled past the video, a lavish animation around a pill followed by the words: *Eliminate Fear!* She spent days scouring for information, but there wasn't much. It was as if she had made the discovery herself. Suddenly, she was Cousteau, Earhart, Salk.

After many consultations, conversations, and some cajoling, her doctor ordered the pill. Now, on her bed, she twisted the ribbon in her hand and heard the doctor's voice, "This medication is unproven. I urge you to reconsider."

But even with the pill in hand, doubts nagged. For a moment, she froze—aren't second thoughts just a fear of the unknown? "Fear," she smiled, then laughed, "in a few hours, there wouldn't be any." She wondered what it might feel like to wake up in the morning and not fear the big or inconsequential things, not fear the future, not fear repeating the past. Would her steps be lighter? Would her thoughts be more focused? Yes, of course, they would!

She flipped open the case, popped the pill into her mouth, and gulped water to wash it down. Quietly, she sat on the bed, feeling nothing. She imagined the pill making its way down her throat into her stomach. Next, it was warming her veins. She could feel her brain being energized by the medicine. As she lay down, her mind raced with visions of the future. Her fingers tapped and danced on the bed.

Tomorrow would be as different as any tomorrow could be.

———

Music to read by: <u>The Gentle Hum of Anxiety</u> by Trent Reznor & Atticus Ross

10. MYRNA AND THE MACHINES

SILICON **V**ALLEY NEVER ASKED **M**YRNA'S **permission.** One day, it just rolled into her little town, all chrome and flashing promises. You probably read about it—a little dot of a town. For a brief time, it became a slightly brighter dot. It was in the papers, and reporters quoted the florist as "confused" by all the fuss. The mayor, reflexively flattening his wispy eyebrows, for the camera, said, "I'm delighted." The head of the PTA said, "We'll let the courts decide" as she held up a hand to keep her face from view.

Myrna said nothing, but oh, the things she heard! As the town's sole ice cream vendor, her shoppe—spelled the old-fashioned way just as she liked it—was a crossroads of chatter. From behind the counter, she'd collect the whispers folks thought they kept quiet—a grumbled complaint, a soon-broken promise, a bit of juicy news. Like coins clattering into the tin she kept on the shelf, the chinwags were her real payment, and more valuable. After all, she won this prized spot with a lucky hand—suited ace-kings against the mayor himself. That allowed her to pull a chit from the tin of secrets she kept above her shoulders. For ten years now, she'd been scooping ice cream rent-free and listening.

Myrna didn't see the first truck roll in late at night. It looked like any ordinary tractor-trailer, except maybe more secretive. The first one had a hoity name: *Omniverge*. Who or what an Omniverge might be was anybody's guess until the doors flung open. Inside were bright, wide aisles full of delicacies from around the world: goat cheese and exotic mushrooms, shiny gadgets, and items with writing that nobody could read. There were places for folks to sit and chit-chat—Myrna preferred the one by the deli. The store had low shelves, so you didn't have to stand on your tippy-toes. Behind a glass wall, a robot chef with whirring arms could cook up a whole Thanksgiving feast in a few hours. The cashiers were friendly, too. They looked almost human. Their smiling faces were just screens that made small talk while scanning your goods at a speedy clip.

The old local market shut down a month or so later, its windows papered over with a brief, "Thank you for all the years" neatly painted on the glass. "Someone must have had their wires crossed, their databases jumbled," the store manager had said. But anywho, there they were, benefactors of sorts, to modernity.

The Omniverge was followed by *Glizen*, a fusion of barber-shop and hair salon. It was automated, too—a whirlwind of chairs on a conveyor, with all sorts of arms swinging from the ceiling. Betty from two doors down called it "marvelous," but it curled some toes, for sure. Myrna had visited, poked around a bit, but preferred to cut her own hair. She wasn't scared of the machine; she just liked the way she could see every snip from her own bathroom mirror.

Some company named *Chiply* built a large wooden play-ground for the kids, complete with a rocking pirate ship. *Tek-*

U-Topia built the surrounding park. For grown-ups who took a sip, platforms with frothy daiquiris would appear with nothing more than a wave. And if you stayed too long, like Myrna did on occasion, a roving nurse was prepared to apply sunscreen with a feather-light touch. In the center of the park was the most interesting fountain she'd ever seen. Jets of water created shapes with aerial acrobatics: a flock of birds, a pair of ice skaters, or a stand of flowers blooming right on cue.

She guessed the tourists started to arrive around then—lookie-loos from other towns in nice cars and no kids. They'd let the multi-story *Rampsy* (or was it *Curbsy*?) car machine nab their car and hoist it up out of the way. They'd wander around, looking in the shops and watching the whiz-gigs do their thing. Most wouldn't shell out a dime for anything except the souvenir t-shirts from the simple vending machine. Some-times, she'd see them stop and gawk at her and the ice cream shoppe. It only made sense they might wonder if she, too, was controlled by a series of computers and satellite uplinks. From behind a book, she'd give them a stiff nod and robotic wink, then fall over laughing when their eyes got big.

Wave upon wave of daily irritants were replaced with beveled-edge bots or screens that hid a mountain of machinery. For every time-sucking blight, there was a new contraption, a new service. "Simple," they said, "easy to use," things destined to unravel the complexities of modern life, each proudly announcing the same lofty promise: freedom. From what, she wondered. But who was she, Myrna, a workaday person in such a lucky town, to turn down the one thing families seemed to crave above all else? Freedom. The whole thing—technology for every problem—was so crafty, so ingenious. And yet, the small talk around her shoppe was more hushed, folks offering fewer smiles.

Indeed, she thought, there had been far less queuing and far more deep, relaxing breaths. Chores in the office or the laundry room were now done by machines that needed no instruction, no sleep. With folks snoring late into the morning, a robot dispenser waited to sprinkle just the right amount of salt on an expertly poached egg. Freedom indeed, they all sighed.

There were some things she really liked about all these upgrades. Like the new *Walkz* system—like a conveyor belt, it took the arthritic hitch out of Myrna's hip while getting around. Well, along with a healthy nip of brandy in her morning tea. But it did pay attention, moving her faster or slower depending on her mood.

The *Sensotek*, that was parlance for movie theater, was another treat...until the food chutes started to malfunction. Myrna found ordering anything with Cheez-Whiz gummed up the works, a sickly-sweet stench filling the air as the whole system shut down.

And those *Bükflyr* drones, she rather liked them. Their constant buzz was a familiar sound as they dropped off books and magazines and whatnot. The convenience was great, but surely there had to be a point where orders couldn't get any faster. Skimming through the manuals, Myrna wondered: do the people who build these systems understand its limits?

And there at the Omni—that's what everyone called the grocery store now—Myrna expected to hear a cheerful bleep. Instead, the terminal returned a disappointing bloop. Then, a clumsy clunk, and it rang out a confusing *dee—eee—eet* before spitting her card out. She sighed and looked at the screen behind the counter as the smiling clerk on the screen faded away. Tilt. Kaput.

Down the street, with her sack crinkling, Myrna stepped onto the self-lowering curb by the elementary school. She held the bag firmly and, with a subtle nudge of her foot, adjusted a loose panel on the mechanical sidewalk as it lurched forward. She stared at the school's open windows, the laughter of children echoing only in her memory. Great glass panes and intricately louvered shades, made to direct wind and sun, now stood askew.

Teachers, as well as books, had become images on portable screens. Changing chapters hardly took more than an eye flick. Children, too, had been given freedom. School could be done from anywhere: the cafeteria, on the lawn, and finally at home. This carried on for a while until curriculum designers justified that children no longer needed to attend school at all... and no one seemed to mind anymore.

Myrna watched the late-arriving tourists who missed the crescendo, their faces pressed against windows, fingers pointing where all that technology once stood. Vagabond sightseers, too, circled the town square but never stopped. That left the streets open for the locals, returning to a rhythm she knew well. And that was fine with Myrna.

The sidewalk stopped to deposit Myrna as she took a deep breath, hoisting the sack to adjust its contents. She steadied herself against the corner, her hand on the sun-warmed brick. A few steps beyond, she knew the whirring machines and blinking sensors had fallen silent. Here, instead, there would be a gathering of expectant eyes, always fewer than some weeks ago. These weren't glassy, unblinking cameras, scanning everything but the soul. These were marbles of blue, brown, and green, creased at the corners with the warmth of genuine smiles. She knew each by name and by heart. Seeing them, a crinkle formed at the corner of her own eyes, her smile as bright as theirs.

Myrna's bag, worn thin, spilled its contents onto the sidewalk. Bags of chocolate and break-proof bottles of marshmallow cream scattered, bouncing and rolling underfoot and over the curb. A dozen or so of her fellow townspeople scuttled about, nabbing each item as Myrna fished her keys from deep in the pocket of her sweater, a small smile tugging at the corner of her mouth. It was much too hot for the frock, but habits are habits, and she expected autumn soon.

With flourished precision they'd seen a thousand times, she pulled the folding glass doors wide open. Her hand reached with a firm grip and pulled a ball at the end of a long rope, sending it snaking high through the bric-a-brac: a tiny tin robot frozen mid-wave, a cracked ray gun from some dime-store vending machine. With a click, a *Bükflyr* drone above whirred to life as a fan, its maker's name sloppily painted over in a rainbow of colors. She flicked a switch, and the back wall blinked to life— OmniVerge screens of smiling virtual clerks with signs taped to each offering: chocolate, vanilla, mango, brandy.

She pulled out a drawer and selected the right set of tools. One big, one small—no electrical cord necessary. The townspeople crowded the counter's edge, their eyes darting, looking at the paraphernalia she'd collected, pretending not to look, but Myrna saw them steal a glance. She didn't mind in the least.

A portable radio clicked to life, a tinny melody from a bygone summer drifting from behind the counter, past the always-fruiting trees beyond.

Myrna smiled as beside her a whirring *Glizen* arm turned and presented the waffle cone dispenser.

Leaning across the counter, she asked, "What'll ya have?"

———

Music to read by: <u>Three to Get Ready</u> by The Dave Brubeck Quartet

11. PIONEERS

"WE'RE CATAPULTED THROUGH THE STARS," HE whistles, a sound that cuts through the bar's hum, more metallic whine than melody. "But the worst part?" His gaze sweeps across the silent, captivated faces of the new recruits. He pauses for effect. "Takeoff!"

He catches his reflection, a boxy shape with a few dings and the surprisingly sharp lines of his attire. He scans the mission patches marking his arms: navigating nebulae around asteroid AR-263, extracting ice from Excelsior 9, the unforeseen rescue of the Njord crew. A flicker of pride softens his features. Why shouldn't he hold court here? Indeed, he was an Atlas, *the* Atlas. An entire cadre had been named for him. He was the prototype, the trailblazer — and after him, the mold was instantly duplicated.

A mechanical hand sets a drink down on the bar, "Thanks, love. Put it on their t-t-tab." He jerks his head, an practiced tick.

"Do I look like I carry a wallet?" he drawls, a hint of self-depre-cation softening the boast. His companions erupt in laughter.

"Anyway, where was I?" He pauses with a hint of wistfulness, "I like being sent first. Are we trailblazers or expendables? Depends on who you ask, I suppose. He shrugs, the motion stiff and mechanical. "But there's a thrill to it, don't you think? We're the first to set eyes on a new world. We're like rockstars, minus the glory..." He sets a hand on the shoulder of a new recruit. "That's our story, you and me, man!"

The attention of the recruits, new to the scene and seemingly just out of the box, clicks with an intensity that captures the room's focus. Any movements cease, making the air still, giving room to his voice.

"The first time I blasted off, I was sure I'd come apart. I felt like I'd end up a bucket of loose parts. It was nothing like the sleek cruisers we have now." He rests his three-fingered hand on the bar, rhythmically tapping.

Leaning back, he recalls, "Back before I was first assembled— what, a dozen cycles ago, we were packed into tiny capsules. Every part of us folded to fit. Launched like cargo. And we mostly were – a limited tool kit and a camera. We'd crash land, roam, and snap a few photos. End of mission."

A flicker of pride passes over his features, momentarily softening the years etched into his surface. "I was proud to be the first to complete a round trip. They had to know we could bring back more than data. We became like settlers with return postage!"

"And, man, even now, when I hit orbit, I get this rush. Batteries charged, motors revving—I'm ready to move!"

His displays brighten, transforming his sturdy form with the excitement of exploration. "There's no feeling quite like being the first to lock treads onto untouched sand, to feel the crunch of alien ice beneath you. To chart the unknown. A thrill only we pioneers truly know. A feel you'll know soon."

As the recruits gather closer, united by shared anticipation, he continues, "Every nut, bolt and wire, will wear smooth with countless miles. While inside, the thrill of discovery burns bright. We may be only gears in the cosmic machine, but we carry the spirit of discovery."

He raises his glass. "And now, as I find my own horizon nears, it's not an ending I face, but a new frontier. One you will explore, forging paths I dared only dream of. This isn't just a legacy...it's a beacon you will amplify, casting light further into than I ever could. Together we stand, not just as tools of exploration, but as the very essence of curiosity and adventure."

With the room hanging on his every word, he concludes, "Remember, the trails we blaze, the worlds we survey, the mysteries we help unravel—these are our mark on the cosmic canvas. We are not just participants in this grand adventure; we are its narrators, born of human ambition, shaped by the stars themselves. We, my friends— from the seasoned to the newly forged — are pioneers."

The recruits stand transfixed, optics wide in wonder, a hum of shared excitement vibrating through the air.

"To the new frontier!" he proclaims.

Their unified response, a chorus that starts as a hum, then vibrates through the station's metal bones. The echo carries outward, weaving through corridors, past flickering displays, until it seems to pierce the station's artificial hull to whisper among the stars.

12. EIGHT MINUTES

"Do you want to watch?" I ask.

"I do," she says, her voice trembling. "...and I don't."

My sister's voice catches as we watch the clock. Her toes curl tight into the blanket, fighting back the fear. I've seen this a hundred times—slow, deep breaths until the panic fades. The others try to mirror her stillness.

I call her sister but, like the rest, she's not blood—circumstance made us family. The five of us, stowaways, left behind by the chaos. When their questions tumble out, I do my best to piece together a past they don't remember—solemn broadcasts, then panic. I try to explain the simple truth: the sun is dying. Soon darkness will be all we know.

Though they listen intently, their dirty faces still register a hope I can't share. These children have known only this dying star and our makeshift family. Each day, we sun ourselves at the edge of the domed roof in the late afternoon until it's safe to slip back inside. In those moments, we savor the breeze and let it fill us. Our eyes study the shapes of the distant mountains until we can describe them from memory.

When they ask, I can't tell them how my senses went numb, hands shaking. Or how my father's body doubled over, retching, until he was only spitting blood. Or how he packed his car in frantic haste, leaving me without a word. I can only paint a vague picture—riots, cities ablaze.

It's then that I remember her, my sister, standing alone, arms up. A tiny figure begging the madness for rescue. We were all alone, I tell them, until we found one another.

Around the world, massive new cities rise up—fortresses built near the bones of the old, designed to protect as life outside will wither. Like Arks meant to save a world, these shelters are a monument to our desperation. Even now, I can feel the blasting in my bones. Canyon-like holes echoed with machinery around the clock as endless lines of earthmovers rattled the old city. Every able hand, every strong back joined the cause.

Inside, it's all false daylight and the timed hiss of manufactured rain. I hear some pay fortunes for a patch of real grass. A whole world paying to pretend nothing's changed. We laugh, picturing their pale faces, as less affluent feet squeak on plastic blades. While outside, the old city bursts with green. Grass and wildflowers poke through every crack, reaching for that dying sun. Inside, they imagine what we touch every day. This wild, forgotten place is our temporary paradise now.

We run full-tilt through the old city, howling like wolves and crazed monkeys in the empty streets. We are the in-betweens, restless missionaries of a forgotten world. Scavengers, we are. We wonder at the absurdity of these buildings left to us. The abandoned skyscrapers still gleam even as vines tear at their crumbling facades. The thoroughfares bathe us in rose, amber, and aqua light. We sniff the fresh air, let it fill us. Each gulp is a precious drink to a wanderer facing a long, parched journey.

Abandoned buildings whisper their secrets, give us their treasures. Over crumbling stairwells, through shattered windows, we dart. Our nimble hands and lithe bodies ignore the empty threats of robot sentries—their metallic chunk-chunk is just a forgotten echo now.

In the silent train station, a young one calls out the Northern Line. I mimic the Southern. Our voices, sharp and clear, ring against the cold marble. Here each of us chooses a destination, faces bright with pretend hope. We know the truth, but this is our play. For a moment, I almost believe.

We each have a specialty—a cook, a gardener, a draftsman, a medic. I'm the teacher and the oldest. My sister is a dancer. Each twirl, a perfect circle in the infinite dust. She bows to our applause, her face alight, as I throw a found bundle of plastic roses at her feet.

Desperate voices from the tunnels ask, "Has it happened?" We don't reply. Like them, we're ghosts now.

Nearly every day from our perch we see them—the ones who will stay outside, clinging to their past. They tend tiny gardens, stubborn patches of green that will never grow to full height. Like ants, they dig their homes deep into the earth. At night, we can see the twinkle of their fires. Do they count the seconds, too? Can they ignore the silent ticking from the clock on the tallest tower? Though it never makes a sound, we hear it in our chests, our heartbeats timed as the numbers fall.

"How long does it take?" my sister asks. She knows the answer. Everyone does.

The sun's light takes a bit over eight minutes to reach us. This is our place to watch, atop the dome, the old and new worlds sprawled at our feet. Far below, specks move and gather on the old city rooftops. People. I hope they are as prepared as we are. This family, these stowaways, we've chosen each other.

As the world braces for the inevitable, we are twisted like stubborn vines, a life built in the high steel of the new city—a home that saved no place for us. Our bodies lean into one another. Behind closed lids, we sear the sun's shape into our minds, feel the whisper of flames, the heat of its core.

My sister and I crouch along the edge, one eye on the countdown. At eight minutes and sixteen seconds, the clock flashes red. A horn shatters the silence. Everywhere, movement stops. The sun is dead, a derelict shape in the vastness of space. From here, the horizon stretches unbroken, our last shadows long and stark. Sister...I don't know where you were born, but to me, you've always been. You, not the clock, are the heartbeat in my dreams. When I imagine the endless night, it's your hand I seek.

I see my sister close her eyes, her face lifted to the last warmth. Our universe takes one last deep breath.

And with a wink, it's gone.

———

Music to read by: <u>Where We're Going</u> by Hans Zimmer

13. SELECTIVE IMMORTALITY

The room echoed with gasps
and burbles, stirring,
Somewhere behind a bench
a stomach was gurgling.
Fingernails flitted,
tapping on metallic rows,
A nervous energy twitched
in legs and in toes.

Everything jittered minutely,
trying to stay still,
Eyes blinked expectantly,
as if with their own will.

They watched as the old man calmly stepped,
His metered strides, now less adept.

As he moved the room was instantly hushed,
The tapping, the gurgling suddenly shushed.
Gooseflesh on arms,
as hair on end did bend,

When the man's head tilted,
his eyes upwardly went.

Grey and bright they lovingly looked,
Through trifocals on a nose,
thin and crook'd.

Up the glass case and into the light,
A deep thump sounded within,
and he filled with delight.
As his hand moved unknowingly
from the side of his face,
And all senses were piqued
in every inch of the space.

Like fish taken from water,
they breathlessly posed,
Rose lips parted,
then closed in hushed repose.

His hand drew a circle
from chest to left breast,
And finished the arc
where his old heart did rest.
His hands shook
and shallow breath strained,
With marvel he noted
what this glass house contained.

A lifetime of toil to make
each and every spare part,
Leading to this—a new human heart.

14. WHEN WE ARRIVE

My brother's tongue hangs out, cracked and dry. I know the sign – a blink and a glance at the sky means he's thirsty. Our mother asked us not to talk very much, so we made our own language with blinks and twitches. She wasn't being curt. It's safer if we stay quiet.

There are three of us; mother, my brother, and me. But our boat has room for four, and I wish father was with us. My brother doesn't understand he isn't coming. We all miss him – Mum most of all, I think. She covers her eyes when she's crying, but I can see her face. We have the same chin, a "matched pair" she says. My brother's dark eyes look like father's, the way he would look at the sky, searching.

I write in this journal every day, sometimes writing the same parts over again so I can remember them. Ink pens are my favorite but all I have is a pencil. Sometimes I start to think about other things, but I always come back to finish my sentences.

We collect rain in a pail for drinking but there hasn't been much lately. The rain flows down the tarpaulin, through a funnel and into a bottle. We always try to keep four bottles full in case we need it since we can't drink the water around our boat. I spilled a bottle once. My brother pretended he did it so I wouldn't get in trouble. He refilled it with seawater and then drank some to show that everything was alright. He got very sick. Since then, he says he's thirsty but won't drink much of the good water. I think he's afraid to get sick again.

My brother and I watch from the front, sinking down into our beds made from bags of belongings. The rest of our things are lashed along the inside of the boat, balancing the weight. During the day, we hide under the canvas tarpaulin for shade. We have to do that a lot recently since there have been no clouds.

Our boat is small but sturdy. My mum steers from the back wearing father's hat low to cover her eyes. I think she likes the hat the best of all our things. It is old and needs to be mended, but I tell her it looks dashing anyway. When I ask my mum where our new home is, she says it's on a future horizon.

My parents built this boat for our family. When the wind is good, we let out the bigger sail and pick up speed. Four to six knots, mother says that's good. Today, we've been moving very fast but I don't know our speed.

———

"Cybelle is strong," I tell her, "she'll take care of her brother"

It's quiet now, early evening when the stars are newest and the fog is yet to roll in. We can't hear the artillery or marching of tanks but we know they're coming. Couriers have reached us from the towns beyond. London, the one we know, is no more. By tomorrow the channel will be full of boats trying to escape. I write these memories, knowing they may be all that's left of our story.

"I can't—," she says to me. Her words drop to the ground with her eyes, followed by her shoulders. We planned for this – she'll take the children and follow our route.

"You're the better sailor…" I say trying to lift her spirits but it's no use, "You are my love, my life–"

Her frame stiffens, eyes set on mine. She gives me a half-smile, repeating our directions from a time when they were just that, "Cracking pace to de la Hague…"

I finish her words, "…then to open ocean."

———

Last week, another boat was on the horizon. My mum used her spyglass but I could see a man when I peeked from under our shade. He looks hunched and tired. As we get close, the man raised an orange flag for us to see. Mother stared at him a good while before telling us it was alright to sit up. My brother held up the orange flag we carry.

My brother blinks asking who the man is. I tell him it's one of us, but I don't recognize him. I remind my brother that we are from all different countries traveling to our new home.

The boats move close to one another, like our paths are going to cross. Our boat makes a much larger wake and causes him to bobble from side-to-side. We use a rope to keep our boats together, then asks us to get some fish and water for the man. Mother keeps a pistol used for flares hidden at her side.

The man asks to join us in our boat since we have extra room. Mother tells him it is best that we do not take on more passengers. This angers the man, who takes the fish and water without saying a word. The man doesn't cook the fish. He pulls large pieces and stuffs them into his mouth. He eats until he's full. Mother, my brother, and I watch him as he washes his face with the ocean water and takes a long, deep drink of the good water from our bottle. He sits back with his eyes closed. With a small burp, he finally says thank you.

The man points his route, his bearing is different from ours. He has directions written inside the wall of his boat. It has been scratched over several times, replaced. I want to tell my mother to show him the map we have, but she has warned us to keep quiet when visitors are near. The man raises his arms and curses at us as he tacks a different route. Mother waits until he's out of sight before we set our sail again.

My father made our map out of leather. I remember my father studying charts for weeks when we moved underground. The oil lamp was barely enough light. Mother's stitches on the map are neat as rows in our vegetable garden. I pretended to sleep as they whispered about the goings-on in London.

We have been on the water for two weeks. That's how long my father has been gone. He stayed to hide our escape and, Mum won't say it, to fight.

The sun plays hide and seek behind the clouds. The wind has changed, making it cooler than recently, even the water seems colder. Mother says it's because we're further from land than ever before. I feel restless today. Mother pushes her hat up and says we're not far. She's in good spirits today. She often sings a hopeful song about our trip, humming the melody and making up funny words.

Far away, mother spots another traveler, she says it's an airship. My brother and I see only a tan bubble above the water. The swells push us closer, and we see a basket of people. They see us too and descend just above the waves. Our ships align with each other but are a football pitch away. We wave to one another.

Mother calls out to them and asks if they have seen anything. At once, they point off in the distance. Mother smiles and tells us that we have been going the right way. The map, the one she and father made, is correct. It's not long now until we reach our new home, she tells us. I think I see tears in her eyes.

My brother and I exchange smiles. We do not have to say anything with blinks to know this news makes us both happy. To be near the end of our journey makes me wonder about our old home.

———

My countrymen, my neighbors, are arm-in-arm as we've taken up positions. While well-fortified we will be no match for their machinery. It's not lost on any of us that we should be so close to Hastings in another battle. This time the invasion isn't from the sea but the heart of our beloved country

———

When we left Fairlight, my brother kept asking about our father. Mum calmly made him be quiet while we set sail. In the dark, I could hear my brother crying. Mother has not told me any more about father, but I am old enough to know he won't be coming to meet us. He and my brother were very close.

Father woke us late, got us dressed. I climbed onto the boat as we had practised, but my brother needed help. He is three years younger than me and still needs some assistance. We kept the sail low until the following day. There weren't any other boats in the channel that time of night, and the water was very still.

Our first day on the boat was exciting. My brother and I stood in the boat because my father had made it very wide and sturdy. We looked out as far as our eyes would let us and could not see land. We know to say port and starboard. My mother taught us to wrap up during daylight to keep our skin from burning. At night, we bundle up in woolen coats and hats that she has made.

Sometimes, we see fish from the boat. Father said we would catch and cook fish to save our other food. Mum always gives us a tangerine for dessert. It tastes like candy. She calls our boat meals adventure food and promises exotic spices to tingle our mouths when our journey ends.

———

The bombardment has begun. My loves, I pray the sun is shining on your faces.

———

It is night. Mother is awake but tired. She sometimes asks me to steer because I am older. I do my best to keep the stars in sight and zig-zag as the wind changes.

My brother is the first to see the lights. Because it is dark, he has to use words, but they come out as squeaks. This wakes mother, who sits up and uses her spyglass. She tells me to continue heading toward them, but we lower the sail so we won't be seen.

Hours pass as we get closer. We lay along our bed, just watching, listening. We are close enough to hear voices now. The voices are talking, laughing. My brother looks at me. It's still dim but I can see his eyes blink with excitement. He makes a grumble-whine sound.

My mother raises our orange flag and lights the lantern so we can be seen. The voices we hear hush one another before a voice calls to us, saying "Ahoy!"

We can make out shapes rising and falling with the swell. As our boat inches closer we see more lanterns directing us. Mother turns us toward them as morning light bounces off a thousand boats! They're made of shiny metal and wood, lashed together like an island. Mother tells us we have found our new home and it's okay to talk now. My brother devours the last of our tangerines, a final taste of home. I want to shout for joy, but something catches in my throat. Instead, I keep quiet.

———

Music to read by: <u>Sons & Daughters</u> by The Decemberists

15. I WIN

7:15 A.M.

The lot doesn't open until 8. The boss arrives 15 minutes early —clockwork, punctual. He'll be driving that shiny Caddy. He'll gently set his thermos on the top as he hikes up his pants, slamming the heavy door. He likes a good old American car. Every day is always the same.

We've had break-ins before—mostly kids trying to boost a stereo or badge from the new model. Nobody breaks in to leave a car, though. She left it here overnight because it's safer. Her sweet, little coupe wouldn't last an hour at my place. I'll put my bag next to hers in the trunk and stash it around the corner. If I can find her key...

25 minutes—

He'll stroll the lot, looking for streaks, maybe a smudge, something the detailers left behind. He'll check his teeth in the chrome after wiping it with a handkerchief, his lips pulled back in that funhouse grin. He'll pick at something, probably his left canine. The gold one. His favorite. That's where his lip curls when he smiles. It always comes out when he's got the upper hand.

I'm inside the lot, scrambling. The key is hidden somewhere safe and "easy to find," she said. It must have fallen somewhere behind a wheel. On the axle? In the rim?

18 minutes. Still time.

It's Tuesday. The skeleton crew, including me, won't show until 8:30. We've put in a weekend haggling over every fee under the sun—we smile, pretend to get approval from the boss, have a cup of coffee, make 'em sweat, come back with a different offer. Rinse, repeat. It's a game. But it's a shitty job from either side of the desk.

When I arrive I'll play it cool. We'll shoot the shit, talk about hustling every schmoe who came in, like always. But I'll be thinking about punching his smug face all day—maybe more than once for each floozy I hide from his wife. Maybe a kick in the balls for each time he slurs the staff and pockets their bonuses. But I won't. I'll take another under-the-table envelope of cash at the end of my shift and see it through. He'll see my middle finger and one last look at my back as I quit. This time I'll leave with a bit more than that skinny envelope.

15 minutes—

I check the tailpipes and run my fingers inside the lip of the rear bumper. The gate is open enough to get one car through if I can find the key. I could push the damned thing out if I had to. Why did she leave it here? Because it's the punchline. The way we planned it. I keep an eye on him while she cleans out everything. That was the deal. We meet up and spend the next week driving through every backwater town toward the border.

Her car can't be here when he arrives. Rounding the corner to the service entrance, he'll spot it. He'll know something is foul. His pace will slow as he gives it a wide berth, taking in the shape. That cruddy little computer in his brain will tally it up. The Etch-a-Sketch will begin to unscramble. The film projector will rewind double-time as he steps closer. Flip goes the Rolodex. And then BAM!

6 minutes—

I see a glint as the sun comes out. The morning fog is burning away and there, wedged between the asphalt and rear driver tire—a silver spec. I dig at it with a pen. I push at the tire to roll the car a fraction of an inch. It loosens. I push it side to side until it's free.

4 minutes—

The car starts and I throw it in gear. I tell myself not to squeal the tires as I slalom between cars on the lot. I'm grinning as I shift, almost to the gate. I can see her running at me, giggling from the park where we'll meet later. She'll throw her head back as I kiss her neck. We'll laugh about his face when he finds the house and bank accounts empty. We won't be able to keep our hands off each other as we speed down the road, the sun at our back.

2 minutes—

Today is going to be a hot one. There's sweat rolling down my face, but I can smell her on my shirt—that cream she uses is unmistakable. In a few hours we'll light him up, send him on the downward spiral. I'll walk right off the lot and the next thing he'll see is his wife's weekend car pull past as I throw the top down. Her vanity plate "*I WIN*" will be the last he'll see of us.

What a schmuck. I'm laughing out loud as I pull to the open gate.

I see the crested badge. And his gold tooth. He slams the heavy door as he steps in my way. He likes good old American cars.

———

Music to read by: <u>Cars</u> by Gary Numan

16. FALLING BACKWARD

THIS WASN'T THE FIRST TIME HIS FEET HAD LOST their grip. The study, worn spines of books, Earth itself tipped over in a great wide arc. When the fall's backward, there's no time. No graceful recovery, just a panicked blink. And then—smack. Flat out.

With a bang, he landed, eyelids fluttering shut. The sudden darkness pulsed with stars, a million pricks against a sea of black. As he lay, his breath rasped in his throat, his hands fumbling at the emptiness.

When the sting of ammonia seared his nostrils, it sent a jolt through him. The chemical blast dragged him from the dark. His fingers twitched, then swatted feebly at the smell. Next, a message arrived for his eyes: open. They obeyed, his left sluggish, the world a blur of harsh light and shifting shapes.

"You've had a fall. Can you hear me?" The voice buzzed in his ears, muffled like a distant radio. Could he hear? Yes. He still hadn't found the volume knob. He nodded, blinked. A fall? Yes to that as well. His bones ached with the memory of it.

A pair of hands—enormous, it seemed—waved something under his nose. Beside them, a face came into focus. Round, worried, with sweat beading on the stubble. One drop broke free, raced down the man's thick sideburn like it was in the Olympics. Funny. He blinked again, the world still swimming. Where the devil was he?

In the periphery... faces, a flash of chrome. This wasn't... where? Before was a void, and now... scattered puzzle pieces. He blinked hard, the world tilting crazily.

He smelled bacon and the musk of shoe polish. When had he last smelled polish? He sat upright. The room clunked to one side, his brain settling into place, he thought. Checkered tiles, a woman's shoes, and the fine hem of a dress. The round man still knelt, his brow furrowed, a hand outstretched.

"Let's get you on your feet," the round man said, pulling him up before moving on to smooth the creases on his own trousers. Friendly eyes, wide with concern, watched from nearby tables. A woman's hand touched his shoulder, gentle, hesitant. Her eyes met his, widening a fraction, a question in them: "Are you alright?" He willed his jaw to move, his lips to curve into a smile. Blinking slowly, he reassured her, "Yes."

He was mostly fine, wasn't he? Fall notwithstanding, of course. His hands brushed his pants, flattened his tie. Familiar motions. He took inventory in this movement—all his limbs seemed to work, senses were more-or-less intact. But why was everyone staring like that?

"I'm sorry, mister," a boy's voice cracked, a jarring counterpoint to the soft murmur of concern. He hadn't seen the boy in his spotless apron or the wet floor. The smell of pine cleaner swirled in his head, sharp and familiar as... as what? His mother's kitchen? Much too long ago for that scent to linger so clearly.

Familiar faces, yes. Neighborly. Familiar, he supposed, in the way magazine ads or old photos often seem. But these people were not picture-perfect like an advertisement. They were flesh and blood, complete with the idiosyncratic details of life: a crooked tie, a cracked tooth, a splatter of burger grease on a sleeve. Yet, there was a smoothness to their appearances that he couldn't quite reconcile. The women had crisp dresses and carefully pinned hair; the men had slicked-back styles and a shine on their shoes. Something unsettled him in the perfection. The light coming in, that golden afternoon light, gave them a Hollywood sheen, like extras. In the murmur of their voices, he listened closely, listening for anything to—

"Maybe we should go?" The woman's voice, soft, kind. A gold locket hung on a chain so thin it could barely be seen against her faded green dress. Like the others, her voice had a lilt, too. Clipped and soft. Midwest? No. He searched the geography in his mind. It was more familiar than anything else in this place but hidden somewhere behind an adjacent thought, just out of reach.

The round man had returned to his work behind the counter. It seemed the show was indeed over for the evening. "No repeat performances tonight, please," he thought to himself.

Outside, the air nipped at his face—a brisk sting. Autumn light, when the sun seemed to linger at the horizon, stretching the seconds as long as time would allow. A time of year for filling the root cellar, for making soup and warm bread. Why did he miss it? She held his elbow, guiding him under the street lamps. As they walked, he looked at the oak and birch leaves laying in dark browns and bright yellow along the sidewalk.

"I think you'll have quite a bump," she said quietly, breaking the trance.

"What happened?" he asked. Her steps beside him faltered for a second.

"Oh, I'm not sure... you just seemed to fall. I think you were leaning and lost your balance."

In the thick of his hair, he felt a knot, a raised, tender lump. His knees throbbed, his elbow ached—stupid, careless fall. In a diner next to a woman he couldn't... couldn't what?

"What were we talking about before I fell?" he asked.

"I'm not sure. Why don't you tell me?" she said.

"That's just it, I seem to have bumped my head hard enough that I've lost a bit of time."

"Well, that's not fair!"

"I know. I'd like to think it was a nice evening. But I can't... can't place it."

"Just give yourself a few minutes."

"The fresh air helps..." His voice trailed off. Was it helping?

Street lamps buzzed as they warmed and began to brighten. She released his elbow, turning to him.

"Do you remember your birthday?" she asked.

"Of course, June sixteenth." A surge of pride, then a small flicker of hesitation. Was that right?

"And your mother's name?"

He pressed his hand to his temple. She tilted her head, that familiar way. The right words hovered, just out of reach. Finally...

"Beatrice. Marie Beatrice," he said, relief flooding him.

"Well, I think you're alright. Any fella who forgets his mother's name..."

"Ask me another."

"Who owns that store?"

He looked where she pointed. The big glass windows were dark, but he could see the outline of the shelves and the newspaper rack. In the back was a single light where an old man shuffled back and forth behind a counter.

"Well, that's Mister Price's pharmacy, of course."

"You see, you haven't lost all your senses. Now, what were we talking about, just before, in the diner?"

He stopped. A cold dread prickled his spine. The woman in the faded green dress... his gaze flickered from her face to the empty street and back. Nothing. His mind, a jumble. There sat a thousand puzzle pieces, refusing to fit. She pursed her lips. Was that a flicker of... anger? No, just concern.

He noticed the moss had grown between the stones, a delicate web of green against the gray. His gaze dropped to his shoes, rocking back on his heels.

"I... I'm sorry," he finally managed. "I just can't..."

Even at twenty paces, he could have seen the disappointment. Close up, it was unbearable. Her entire shape had slowly changed in front of him like a flower closing as the sky darkened.

"I'm not feeling well," she said, in nearly a whisper.

From her small handbag, she pulled a scarf. Delicate, the same faded green as her dress. It settled around her shoulders, and still, the locket gleamed against her skin.

"Let me walk you," he offered.

"I can manage. My mother..." Her voice faded, the weight of it settling between them.

He didn't... couldn't find the words. He felt the same weight that pressed on her shoulders pushing them both to the ground. Another piece, somewhere just out of sight. He wanted to scream, to grab those fragments, force them to make sense.

She stepped further away, heels ticking on the brickwork. But he saw it then: she was the missing tile, the single perfect fit.

"I'd give anything to see you again," he said, his voice unsteady.

"If you remember, come find me tomorrow," she said. Her hand brushed the gold chain, quietly adding, "Even if you don't..."

Her footsteps fading in the night, disappearing as she rounded the corner.

Night steals the fading day. A car cuts through the dusk, its headlights washing over him. He turns, shielding his eyes, watches her silhouette disappear. In a darkened window, a figure flickers—strangely familiar.

He barely recognized him—the young man staring back from the darkened window. A neatly pressed suit, a jaunty pocket square... familiar, yet distant. A hesitant wave fluttered from his hand. The figure in the window mirrored the gesture. He straightened his own tie, a spark of old habit. The figure moved with him, hand dipping into a pocket as his own did. A rabbit's foot jangled—and a box?

Inside, black velvet and a flash of gold. This was it—the missing piece! This belonged on the hand of the woman in the pale green dress. Seeing it fully, the ring captured all the stars, magnifying them as every other light dimmed, bowing. His hand moved to hold it up, to show her what he had found. Out of the box it tumbled, rolling free. His young eyes watched it bounce over the bricks.

He lunged for the ring, his fingers fumbling, desperate. His heart raced. A surge of what? Joy? No, something... important. But his polished shoes betrayed him, slipping on the moss. Plummeting. The Earth's gravity pulling him down. Until, smack. Flat out. And just like that, the stars were a fading curtain at the edge of his vision.

He lay there, a jumble in his head. Fragments of the puzzle lay apart, still not complete. The hum, always the hum. Bacon... was she cooking again?

Eyes opened. Bookshelves loomed, out of place somehow. A hand on his arm, frail. A woman's face, a flicker of something familiar, faded, incomplete. He moved his shoulders, still working, he thought. And wiggled his toes—they were cold.

"Let's get you on your feet," a familiar voice said. The world shifted into place as he stood. His head throbbed. Knees and elbows, too. Casualties of entropy, he thought.

The woman's hand on his shoulder, gentle, hesitant. Her eyes met his, widened a fraction. A question in them: "Are you alright?" His eyes found the gold locket on a chain that looked too thin to hold it.

She looked at him, tilting her head in a way that was both strange and achingly familiar.

———

Music to read by: "<u>Indian Summer</u>" by Glenn Miller

17. SOULSIGHT

Pop! A champagne cork flies through the air, tumbling out of sight.

A dozen people stand in an otherwise empty office. Take-out cartons lay everywhere. Bottles, cans, red plastic cups. Somewhere in the sea of cubicles music is playing. The clock on a screensaver bounces around the screen: 2:07am.

A staffer enters, setting a six pack of beer on a desk, and a package, "Courier left this outside."

"Oh, what do we have here?" A woman says, ripping open the parcel. Inside is a freshly printed copy of Fortune magazine.

On the cover: Gregory — a young man, early 30s, surrounded by data servers. The look on his face is confident, maybe a bit smug.

"Not another..." Gregory says. His hand waving in mock humility.

"Let's read a bit, shall we?" She says, flipping pages to find the article, "The headline....'*Inventor Turns Tech Inward, Says: I've Found the Soul*'"

"They changed the title," someone says.

"Should I keep reading?"

Hoots, claps, a "fuck yeah!"

The woman clears her throat and begins...

"In a breathtaking advancement that blurs the lines between technology and the metaphysical, Gregory Bledel, a pioneering inventor in artificial intelligence, claims to have developed a way to not just visualize but dynamically replay the essence of the human soul. His new technology, SoulSight, utilizes cutting-edge neural imaging and sophisticated machine learning algorithms to offer users a replay of significant life events from their soul's perspective.

From his recognition as a tech prodigy..."

"Prodigy?"

Gregory smiles, palm to forehead, feigning embarrassment.

"...Bledel has always pushed the boundaries of what technology can achieve. With SoulSight, he takes a bold step into the realm of human consciousness, proposing that it's possible to access and visualize one's deepest emotional experiences. 'This system isn't just a tool for reflection; it's a bridge to the deeper self, a way to literally view your life through the lens of your soul,' Bledel explains."

"Should I go on?"

"...Individuals who have experienced the SoulSight Replay describe it as transformative, providing unprecedented insight into their emotional and psychological makeup. 'It's a revelation, seeing your most poignant moments replayed with such clarity and emotion. It's like reliving them with a new sense of understanding,' says one user."

"They quoted your sister?"

Gregory laughs, nods, takes a sip.

The reading continues...

"...raises profound ethical questions, particularly concerning the privacy and security of sensitive personal data. The technology's capability to access and display one's innermost experiences calls for rigorous oversight. Dr. Lena Thorpe..."

"Boo!" says someone.

"...a leading ethicist at the Technology and Ethics Group, emphasizes the need for stringent regulations. 'While the potential of such technology is vast, the privacy implications are enormous. We must tread carefully to ensure that innovations like SoulSight do not compromise individual privacy or autonomy,' she warns."

SoulSight Data Breach Reveals Career-Ending Secrets of Elite Users

Just six months after the debut of the groundbreaking SoulSight technology, which promised a revolutionary way to visualize and replay personal emotional experiences, the platform is grappling with a catastrophic data breach.

Among the victims of this breach are prominent business leaders, political figures, and celebrities who were among the first to adopt this innovative technology. The leaked data—detailed replays of their private SoulSight sessions—reveals highly sensitive personal reactions and decisions that were never meant for public consumption. This includes a session from a top executive from NexInnovate Solutions (NXS), who was recorded expressing relief at the news of the former CEO's untimely death.

This revelation has not only sparked a fierce public backlash but also led to a significant drop in NXS's stock as investors and stakeholders question the ethical standing of its leadership....

SoulSight Unveils Digital Amnesia Service in Wake of Data Breach

In a bold move that mixes innovation with controversy, SoulSight Technologies has introduced a new service aimed at combating the fallout from their recent high-profile data breach: the Digital Amnesia Service. This pioneering solution promises to erase specific memories related to the breach, offering peace of mind to affected users and anyone who inadvertently viewed sensitive leaked data.

The launch was announced through a sleek, well-orchestrated media campaign, showcasing testimonials from relieved users and detailing the sophisticated neural technology behind the service. "In these challenging times, our priority remains the emotional and mental well-being of our users," stated Gregory Bledel, CEO of SoulSight. "The Digital Amnesia Service is our commitment to restoring privacy and tranquility to those affected by this unprecedented breach..."

Hackers Exploit SoulSight's Digital Amnesia Technology for Nefarious Purposes

SoulSight Technologies, once celebrated for its revolutionary Digital Amnesia Service designed to help victims of a data breach, now finds itself at the center of a new controversy. Reports have emerged that hackers are exploiting the technology, using it for yet-to-be-fully-understood malicious purposes, raising alarm across cybersecurity and ethical domains.

"The potential for abuse of memory-altering technology is something we've long feared," stated cybersecurity expert Helena Forsyth. "It's a powerful tool that, if misused, can lead to unknown consequences, not just for the individuals targeted but for society at large." Reports indicate that hackers may be using the technology to erase memories of their own illegal activities from witnesses or victims, essentially 'cleaning' the slate of any who might recall their crimes...

Gregory Bledel: From Tech Visionary to President in a Historic Landslide Victory

In an unprecedented shift from Silicon Valley to the corridors of power tin Washington, D.C., Gregory Bledel, the charismatic founder and CEO of SoulSight Technologies, has been elected President of the United States in a landslide victory. Voters across the nation were captivated by Bledel's vision, charm, and his seemingly innate ability to connect with the common person on a human level.

Bledel's journey from a tech mogul to the highest office in the land sounds like the plot of a Hollywood movie, yet it is the reality Americans woke up to today. His campaign, which some initially viewed with skepticism given his corporate background, quickly gained momentum as he toured the country. Bledel's speeches, filled with optimism and a clear vision for a technology-driven future, resonated deeply with a populace eager for innovation and sincerity in politics.

"Gregory Bledel brings more than just successful business acumen to the table; he brings a sense of hope and a promise of integrity," remarked political analyst Maria Gonzales. "His campaign was remarkably free of the usual political rhetoric, focusing instead on substantive, achievable goals."

As President-elect Bledel prepares to take office, the world watches with bated breath, hopeful that his tenure will be marked by the same innovation and integrity that defined his campaign. Whether he will transform the political landscape with the same effectiveness with which he revolutionized technology remains to be seen. But for now, Gregory Bledel stands as a symbol of change, the very embodiment of a new American dream shaped by silicon circuits and human heartstrings alike...

18. MISSUS TOM

"I miss you," she says quietly. At this very window, she'd sit for hours, not moving, her eyes searching the heavens. Out there was the rural sky, so full of stars, and him.

This was better than the city with its noisy crowds and department stores. All those televisions flickering into the late hours. City people simply couldn't see the stars, not like she could now. The swishes of light seemed brighter on damp autumn evenings, didn't they?

She remembered listening to him tell the story of his upcoming transit with such precision. Nightly, stories were coaxed from him, even though she knew them all beat-by-beat. It was his voice she wanted to hear—so clear, so measured in cadence. He'd raise his long fingers, point out the Gods and their lesser constellations, and say their names with such reverence.

She knew that out there, he would pause and look back. With his visor down to block the brilliant sun, he'd see the Earth as a tiny drop of blue, getting ever smaller. In time, he'd only be able to imagine the place he once called home. But she understood that this dirt and rock were transient for him. His life was meant to be lived somewhere deep, beyond the charted cosmos. She wanted that for him.

With a squint into the void, she imagined him out there, alone in his tin can—tumbling and floating. For a moment, she felt as if she could see him, daring to push further from reach. She paused, the thought both thrilling and terrifying.

His voice was thin but firm as the radio waves carried a last message, *"Tell my wife I love her very much."*

She knew.

———

Music to read by: Space Oddity by David Bowie